CHRISTMAS JOKES

FOR

FUNNY KIDS

HUNDREDS OF HILARIOUS JOKES INSIDE!

JIMMY JONES

Hundreds of really funny, hilarious Christmas jokes that will have the kids in fits of laughter in no time!

They're all in here - the funniest
- Christmas Jokes
- Christmas Riddles
- Christmas Tongue Twisters
- Christmas Knock Knock Jokes

for Funny Kids!

Funny kids love funny jokes and this brand new collection of original and classic Christmas jokes promises hours of fun for the whole family!

Books by Jimmy Jones

Funny Jokes For Funny Kids
Knock Knock Jokes For Funny Kids
Christmas Jokes For Funny Kids

Funny Jokes For Kids Series
All Ages 5 -12!

To see all the latest books by Jimmy Jones just go to
kidsjokebooks.com

Contents

Christmas Jokes!

What did the snowman wear
to his wedding?

His snowsuit!

What did the cow say on January the 1st?

Happy Moo Year!

What do you call a Christmas toy that
does nothing all day long?

An inaction Figure!

What did Santa's dog say when he sat on sandpaper?

Ruff!

What do you call your dad when he is covered in snow?

Pop-sicle!

Why didn't the elephant waiter get paid much at the Christmas dinner?

He was working for peanuts!

What is Santa's dog called?

Santa Paws!

Why is it so cold at Christmas?

It's Decembrrrrrrr!

If a reindeer is born in Canada, grows up
in Australia and dies in America,
what is he?

Dead!

What do you get if you cross a boomerang with a Christmas present?

A gift that returns itself!

What is Santa's cat called?

Santa Claws!

What did the frog have for Christmas lunch?

A diet croak with french flies!

What kind of paper likes singing
at Christmas?

Wrapping paper!

What is green, white and red and
lays on the beach?

A sunburnt elf!

Which insects love the snow?

Mo-ski-toes!

What do you call a lying snowman?
A snow fake!

Why was the elf onstage
at the concert?
He is really good at wrapping!

What did the astronaut drink
after Christmas lunch?
A nice cup of gravi-tea!

How can you learn how to make
a Christmas banana split?

Go to sundae school!

Why does Santa wear 3 pairs of pants
when he plays golf?

In case he gets a hole in one!

What did Santa say to the
stressed snowman?

Chill out, dude!

Why did the swimmer stop swimming
at Christmas?

The sea weed!

What do you call a snowman on a
hot day?

Puddle!

What did Santa do in his
vegetable patch?

Hoe, Hoe, Hoe!

What do you call a man who claps
at Christmas?

Santa-plause!

Who brought Christmas presents
to baby sharks?

Santa Jaws!

Why was the elf always late for
Elf school?

They kept ringing the bell

before he got there!

Why did Santa get a didgeridoo
for Christmas?

To answer the phone if

the boomerang!

What is red and white, red and white,
red and white?

Santa rolling down the stairs!

What happened to Santa's cat when she
ate 3 lemons?

She became a sour puss!

Which reindeer got into trouble for not being polite?

Rude-olph!

What did Adam say on the night before Christmas?

It's Christmas, Eve!

Why did Santa call his dog 'Frost'?

Frost bites!

Why did the tissue dance all night long on Christmas eve?
It was full of boogey!

What did the snowman eat for his breakfast?
Frosted Flakes!

What did Santa's cat eat for Christmas dessert?
Mice cream!

What do you call it when Santa's helper takes a photo of himself?

An Elfie!

Why did Santa's cat jump up on the computer?

So she could catch the mouse!

What game to tornadoes play at Christmas parties?

Twister!

What did Santa's dog say to the flea?

Stop bugging me!

Why did the butterfly leave the
Christmas dance?

It was a moth ball!

What do snowmen sing on
their birthday?

Freeze a jolly good fellow,

freeze a jolly good fellow!

Why did Santa Claus get his sleigh
for free?

It was on the house!

Which elf sang the best songs?

Elf-is Presley!

Why did the snowman wear
a bow tie?

To go to the snowball!

What did the Elf get treated for when his computer bit him?

A Megabyte!

What do elves love learning the most at school?

The elf-abet!

Where did the ghost go for his Christmas holiday?

Mali-booo!

What happens if Santa's dog eats too much garlic?

His bark is worse than his bite!

What do you call a vampire Santa Claus?

Sackula!

Why did the reindeer cross the road?

The chicken had the day off!

Why did the Reindeer's toilet paper
roll down the hill?

To get to the bottom!

How do snowmen get to work?

On their icicle!

What happened to the girl who ate
the Christmas decorations?

She got Tinsell-itus!

Why did the penguin skip her first day at work?
She got cold feet!

What fast food do snowmen eat?
Iceberg-ers!

Where do bees go for their Christmas holiday?
Stingapore!

What has 4 legs, a trunk and
wears sunglasses?

A mouse on her Christmas vacation!

What Mexican food is best on a
really cold day?

Brrrr-itos!

How do snowmen learn things?

They go on the winternet!

Which month of the year do
Christmas trees hate?

Sep-Timberrr!

Why don't crabs give out
Christmas presents?

They are too shellfish!

What does Santa's dog love to eat
for breakfast?

Pooched eggs!

What instrument can Santa's dog play?

The Trom-Bone!

What is the funniest part of
Christmas day?

The laughternoon!

Why did the mushroom go to the
Christmas party?

He was a fungi (fun guy)!

Why did he leave the Christmas party?

There wasn't mush room!

Who hid in the bakery on
Christmas Eve?

The mince spy!

What do birds send out at Christmas?

Tweets!

How did Santa's dog stop the
video from playing?

By pressing the paws button!

What do you call a snowman who has been sunbaking for a week?

Water!

What exercise did Santa's cat do in the morning?

Puss Ups!

What did Santa Claus get for Easter?

Jolly Beans!

Why do the fastest reindeers go
to McDonalds at Christmas?

To get some fast food!

Why did the reindeer say
Mooooo?

She was learning another

language!

If you are really cold and grumpy
at Christmas what do you eat?

A brrrgrrr!

What do you call a polar bear
in the desert?

Lost!

What is a skunk's favorite
Christmas song?

Jingle smells, jingle smells!

What do you call Santa's dog in
the snow?

A Pup-Sicle!

Why do birds fly south at Christmas?
It's way too far to walk!

What do you call a snowman
on a skateboard?
A snow mobile!

What did the vampire get when he
bit the snowman?
Frostbite!

What do you call a snowman
with dandruff?

Snowflakes!

What did Mrs Claus say to Santa Claus
when she looked out the window?

It looks like rain, dear!

Why did the lady wear a helmet
to Christmas dinner?

She was on a crash diet!

Why couldn't the cross eyed Elf teacher get a job?

She couldn't control her pupils!

What do you call a very rich elf?

Welfy!

What did the snowman eat for a morning snack?

Snowflakes!

Christmas Knock Knock Jokes!

Knock knock.

Who's there?

Sister.

Sister who?

Sister right place for the Christmas party tonight?

Knock knock.

Who's there?

Claire.

Claire who?

Claire the way! Rudolph's here!

Knock knock.

Who's there?

Beth.

Beth who?

Beth friends stick together so can you give me your presents?

Knock knock.

Who's there?

Honda.

Honda who?

Honda first day of Christmas my true love sent to me...!

Knock knock.

Who's there?

Harmony.

Harmony who?

Harmony presents did you get?

I've got 7!

Knock knock.

Who's there?

Alpaca.

Alpaca who?

Alpaca all my presents into

my suitcase.

Can you give me some of yours too?

Knock knock.

Who's there?

Noah.

Noah who?

Noah good place to hide my presents?

How about in the closet!

Knock knock.

Who's there?

Stella.

Stella who?

Let's Stella 'nother Christmas joke!

Ho! Ho! Ho!

Knock knock.

Who's there?

Mary and Abby.

Mary and Abby who?

Mary Christmas and a

Abby New Year!

Knock knock.

Who's there?

Zinc.

Zinc who?

I zinc chocolate is tastier

than broccoli!

Knock knock.

Who's there?

Wooden Shoe.

Wooden shoe who?

Wooden shoe know it!

Santa is here! Yayyyyy!

Knock knock.

Who's there?

Juicy.

Juicy who?

Juicy the news! 3 snowmen

moved in next door!

Knock knock.

Who's there?

Sonia.

Sonia who?

Sonia shoe! Melted chocolate!

Ewwww!

Knock knock.

Who's there?

Sadie.

Sadie who?

Sadie magic word and Santa

will appear!

Knock knock.

Who's there?

Ahmed.

Ahmed who?

Ahmed a mistake! Sorry!

Wrong house for the

Christmas party!

Knock knock.

Who's there?

Bean.

Bean who?

Bean waiting here for ages! Why

are you always late for Christmas?

Knock knock.

Who's there?

Vitamin.

Vitamin who?

Vitamin for the Christmas party!

He's a lot of fun!

Knock knock.

Who's there?

Freeze.

Freeze who?

Freeze a jolly good fellow!

Freeze a jolly good fellow!

Knock knock.

Who's there?

Alby.

Alby who?

Alby back in a minute, so just wait there while I ride my new bike!

Knock knock.

Who's there?

Accordion.

Accordion who?

Accordion to the radio, Rudolph theReindeer will be here in 5 minutes!

Knock knock.

Who's there?

Betty.

Betty who?

Betty you can't guess how many gifts I have? 14! Yayyyy!

Knock knock.

Who's there?

Rabbit.

Rabbit who?

Rabbit up neatly please. It's a Christmas present!

Knock knock.

Who's there?

Raymond.

Raymond who?

Raymond me to bring more candy canes next time! Yummy!

Knock knock.

Who's there?

Cher.

Cher who?

Cher would like to meet Santa Claus. Do you have his address?

Knock knock.

Who's there?

Cupid.

Cupid who?

Cupid quiet!

I'm trying to sneak up on Rudolph!

Shhhh.

Knock knock.

Who's there?

Ketchup.

Ketchup who?

Let's ketchup later on and

play XBox!

Knock knock.

Who's there?

Arthur.

Arthur who?

Arthur any more presents for me?

Come on! Just 1 more!

Knock knock.

Who's there?

Alaska.

Alaska who?

Alaska you one more time!

Please tell me where

Santa Claus lives!

Knock knock.

Who's there?

Needle.

Needle who?

Needle hand to eat your cake?

I'm still hungry!

Knock knock.

Who's there?

Emma.

Emma who?

Emma very hungry!

How about candy canes for lunch?

Knock knock.

Who's there?

Thumb.

Thumb who?

Thumb presents fell off the porch!

Noooooo!

Knock knock.

Who's there?

Dozen.

Dozen who?

Dozen anybody want to give me

some candy?

I'm starving!

Knock knock.

Who's there?

Troy.

Troy who?

Troy to get some Christmas cake before grandpa eats it all!

Knock knock.

Who's there?

Izzy.

Izzy who?

Izzy Christmas lunch still on? I took 4 buses to get here!

Knock knock.

Who's there?

Lettuce.

Lettuce who?

Please lettuce in before

Santa gets here!

Knock knock.

Who's there?

Snow.

Snow who?

Snow business like show business!

Knock knock.

Who's there?

Abby.

Abby who?

Abby New Year!

Let's celebrate!

Knock knock.

Who's there?

Mint.

Mint who?

I mint to tell you - I ate all of your Christmas cake!

Knock knock.

Who's there?

Carmen.

Carmen who?

Carmen get your candy!

Candy for sale! Great prices!

Knock knock.

Who's there?

Norma Lee.

Norma Lee who?

Norma Lee I get full from 1 candy cane but today I've had 3!

Knock knock.

Who's there?

Gladys.

Gladys who?

Gladys Christmas!

Let's party!

Knock knock.

Who's there?

Fiddle.

Fiddle who?

Fiddle make you happy I'll keep

telling Christmas jokes!

Knock knock.

Who's there?

Waiter.

Waiter who?

Waiter I tell your mom!

You ate 15 candy canes!

Knock knock.

Who's there?

Pasta.

Pasta who?

It's way Pasta your bedtime!

Lucky we stay up late

at Christmas!

Knock knock.

Who's there?

Athena.

Athena who?

Athena reindeer in your back yard!

Come and see!

Knock knock.

Who's there?

Reindeer.

Reindeer who?

It looks like rain, deer!

Knock knock.

Who's there?

Wayne.

Wayne who?

It's going to Wayne! Quick!

Let's move the party inside!

Knock knock.

Who's there?

Udder.

Udder who?

You look a bit Udder the weather!

Did you eat too much

Christmas cake?

Knock knock.

Who's there?

Harry.

Harry who?

Harry up!

Santa has been! Woohoo!

Knock knock.

Who's there?

Zookeeper.

Zookeeper who?

Zookeeper way from my candy cane!

I need it for my lunch tomorrow!

Knock knock.

Who's there?

Avon.

Avon who?

Avon you to show me where you hid your presents!

Knock knock.

Who's there?

Hannah.

Hannah who?

Hannah partridge in a pear tree!

Knock knock.

Who's there?

Jamaican.

Jamaican who?

Jamaican Christmas dinner?

Yummy!

Knock knock.

Who's there?

Van.

Van who?

Van are you going to let me in?

It's Christmas!

Knock knock.

Who's there?

Funnel.

Funnel who?

Funnel start in just a minute!

Christmas time! I love it!

Knock knock.

Who's there?

Yule.

Yule who?

Yule never know if you don't

open the door!

Knock knock.

Who's there?

Wilfred.

Wilfred who?

Wilfred be able to help me open

my presents?

I heard he's an expert!

Knock knock.

Who's there?

Zany.

Zany who?

Zany way we can fit all these

presents into my car?

Knock knock.

Who's there?

Weirdo.

Weirdo who?

Weirdo you think all these

presents came from?

The Easter Bunny?

Knock knock.

Who's there?

Irish.

Irish who?

Irish I knew where the biggest

present is hidden!

Christmas Riddles!

What do you call a girl snowman?
A snow Ma'am!

How many presents can Santa fit
into an empty sack?
One. After that it's not empty!

What kind of egg is nice to drink?
Eggnog!

What would Santa be called if he lost his underwear?

Saint Knicker-less!

Where do reindeers go if they lose their tails?

A re-tail shop!

What do you call a quiet man in a suit of armor?

A silent knight!

What is a wolf's favorite
Christmas song?
Deck the howls!

Where do they film movies
about Christmas?
Tinsel Town!

Where does Santa store his clothes?
In his Claus-et!

What did the snow woman do to the snowman after an argument?

Gave him the cold shoulder!

Which kind of toe is not on your foot?

Mistletoe!

When does Santa go exactly as fast as a train?

When he's on the train!

What side of a reindeer has
the most fur?

The outside!

What do reindeers hang on the
Christmas tree?

Hornaments!

What did Santa eat for a snack?

A peanut butter and jolly sandwich!

What happens after all the gifts for Christmas have been opened?

Christmess!

What did the snowman eat at the fair?

A snowcone!

What is worse than finding an insect when you are eating Christmas cake?

Finding half an insect!

What's the best thing to put into a yummy Christmas cake?

Your teeth!

How do you decorate a row boat for Christmas?

Oar-naments!

What do you call a deep fried Santa?

Crisp Kringle!

If the end of the year is at the end of December, what is at the end of Christmas?

The letter 's'!

What game did the reindeers play in their barn?

Stable tennis!

Why did the girl take her ruler to bed on Christmas eve?

To see how long Santa would be!

How do angels greet each other?
Halo!

What did prehistoric reindeers use to cut down trees?
A dino-saw!

Where did Santa learn to swim?
The North Pool!

What do you get when you cross a bird with a turtle?

A turtle dove!

What did the doctor say to the Christmas bell when it was sick?

If you're not better in 2 days give me a ring!

How did the snow globe feel on Christmas day?

A bit shaken!

What sort of ball doesn't bounce?
A snowball!

What did Santa use after he hurt one of his legs?
A candy cane!

Why did the girl throw her Christmas calendar out the window?
So the days would fly by!

What gets chopped down, stood up and has a star on top?

A Christmas tree!

Why did Santa get a parking ticket?

He parked the sleigh in a

Snow Parking Zone!

What do you get if you cross a detective with Saint Nick?

Santa Clues!

Christmas

Tongue Twisters!

Tongue Twisters are great fun!
Start off slow.
How fast can you go?

Santa stacked six sleighs.
Santa stacked six sleighs.
Santa stacked six sleighs.

Green glass globes glow greenly.
Green glass globes glow greenly.
Green glass globes glow greenly.

Santa's sack slowly sags.
Santa's sack slowly sags.
Santa's sack slowly sags.

Snow slows Santa's sleigh.
Snow slows Santa's sleigh.
Snow slows Santa's sleigh.

Kris Kringle climbs quickly.
Kris Kringle climbs quickly.
Kris Kringle climbs quickly.

Red lolly, yellow lolly.
Red lolly, yellow lolly.
Red lolly, yellow lolly.

Clever Claire cuts Christmas cards.
Clever Claire cuts Christmas cards.
Clever Claire cuts Christmas cards.

Santa's sleigh slid sideways.
Santa's sleigh slid sideways.
Santa's sleigh slid sideways.

Fred fed Ted bread.
Fred fed Ted bread.
Fred fed Ted bread.

Boat toy boat toy boat toy.
Boat toy boat toy boat toy.
Boat toy boat toy boat toy.

Billy builds big blocks.
Billy builds big blocks.
Billy builds big blocks.

Seven sleepy Santas sang songs.
Seven sleepy Santas sang songs.
Seven sleepy Santas sang songs.

Santa sang seven slow songs.
Santa sang seven slow songs.
Santa sang seven slow songs.

Bakers bake bright blue bells.
Bakers bake bright blue bells.
Bakers bake bright blue bells.

Santa slowly shines shoes.
Santa slowly shines shoes.
Santa slowly shines shoes.

Santa slowly stuffs six striped stockings.
Santa slowly stuffs six striped stockings.
Santa slowly stuffs six striped stockings.

Stuffed Santa Sleeps Silently.
Stuffed Santa Sleeps Silently.
Stuffed Santa Sleeps Silently.

Six slippery snowmen slide.
Six slippery snowmen slide.
Six slippery snowmen slide.

Eleven elves licked little lollipops.
Eleven elves licked little lollipops.
Eleven elves licked little lollipops.

Ten tiny tin trains.
Ten tiny tin trains.
Ten tiny tin trains.

Three free trees.
Three free trees.
Three free trees.

How many deer would a reindeer reign
if a reindeer could reign deer?
How many deer would a reindeer reign
if a reindeer could reign deer?
How many deer would a reindeer reign
if a reindeer could reign deer?

Silly snowman slips and slides.
Silly snowman slips and slides.
Silly snowman slips and slides.

Bonus

Christmas Jokes!

What do cats sing at Christmas?
We wish you a furry Christmas

and a Happy Meow Year!

What do you call Santa's dog when
she has a fever?
A hot dog!

What did the cow say to the sheep
on Christmas day?
Moooo-ry Christmas!

Why didn't the boy like his
Christmas present of a wooden car
with a wooden engine?

It wooden go!

Why do owls love going to
Christmas parties?

They are always such a hoot!

What does Santa take for bad breath?

Orna-mints!

Why did Santa have so much facial hair?

Not sure but it seemed to

just grow on him!

Where do cows go on their day off
at Christmas?

The Moooo-seum!

What time is it when a reindeer
sits on your lunch box?

Time to get a new lunch box!

What is the wettest animal?
A rain-deer!

What did one snowman say to the other?
It's ice to see you again!

Why was the elf so shy?
She had low elf-esteem!

How did Santa feel when he got stuck in a chimney?

Claus-trophobic!

What did Santa's cat say when Santa stepped on its tail?

Me-owww!

What did the doctor give the sick snowman?

Chill pills!

What do you call a white bear at
the North Pole?
A Polar Brrrrr!

Where did Santa stay on vacation?
In a Ho Ho Ho-tel!

What did the policeman say to the
robber snowman?
Freeze!

What did one snowman say
to the other?

Can you smell carrots?

What song does Tarzan love
at Christmas?

Jungle Bells!

Why did the chicken play the drums
at the Christmas concert?

She already had the drumsticks!

What do elves have that nothing else in the entire world has?

Baby elves!

Why did the boy take 3 rolls of toilet paper to the Christmas party?

He was a party pooper!

How did Santa defeat the evil Dragon?

He sleigh-ed it!

What do you call a poor Santa?
Saint Nickel-less!

Who delivers presents to the beach?
Sandy Claus!

When is the best time to buy a
bird for a Christmas gift?
When they are going cheep!

Who is never hungry at Christmas?
The turkey because he is

totally stuffed!

What did the vampire put on his
Christmas dinner?
Grave-y!

What kind of Christmas books do
skunks read?
Best Smellers!

What did the snowman say after his eye operation?

I-cy!

Where does Santa keep his money?

In the snowbank!

What do you call a woman who only sings at Christmas?

Carol!

How do you know if a reindeer has been living in your refrigerator?

There are footprints

in the butter!

Why did the cow wear a bell on the way to Christmas lunch?

Her horn didn't work!

Where do you find a reindeer with one nose, two ears, one tail but no legs?

Exactly where you left him!

Bonus Christmas Knock Knock Jokes!

Knock knock.

Who's there?

Turnip.

Turnip who?

Turnip the music! Let's party!

Knock knock.

Who's there?

Andrew.

Andrew who?

Andrew a very nice picture of Santa!

Knock knock.

Who's there?

Chicken.

Chicken who?

I'm chicken under the Christmas tree and I can't find any presents! Noooo!

Knock knock.

Who's there?

CD.

CD who?

CD leftover Christmas cake? That's my lunch for tomorrow!

Knock knock.

Who's there?

Myth.

Myth who?

I myth Christmas tho much!

How about you?

Knock knock.

Who's there?

Seymour.

Seymour who?

I Seymour presents when I

wear my glasses!

Knock knock.

Who's there?

Zesty.

Zesty who?

Zesty right place for the Christmas party?

Knock knock.

Who's there?

Mushroom.

Mushroom who?

Do you have mushroom left in your Christmas stocking? Mine is full!

Knock knock.

Who's there?

Army.

Army who?

Army and you still going to share our candy? Yummy!

Knock knock.

Who's there?

Elsa.

Elsa who?

Who Elsa do you think it would be? Father Christmas?

Knock knock.

Who's there?

Witches.

Witches who?

Witches the best way to get a photo of Santa?

Knock knock.

Who's there?

Ken.

Ken who?

Ken you give me a hand with this present? It weighs 100 pounds!

Knock knock.

Who's there?

Dish.

Dish who?

Dish is the best Christmas present

I have ever seen!

Knock knock.

Who's there?

Tweet.

Tweet who?

Would you like tweet some candy?

Yummy!

Knock knock.

Who's there?

Santa.

Santa who?

Santa Christmas card to you but you didn't send one to me!

Knock knock.

Who's there?

Harvey.

Harvey who?

I hope you Harvey very good Christmas my good friend!

Knock knock.

Who's there?

Bat.

Bat who?

Bat you will never guess who gave

me this candy?

Aunt Betty!

Knock knock.

Who's there?

Felix.

Felix who?

Felix my Christmas cake one more

time he can get me a new one!

Knock knock.

Who's there?

Pudding.

Pudding who?

Pudding cake in your mouth!

Open wide!

Knock knock.

Who's there?

Summer.

Summer who?

Summer my friends don't like

candy. I love it!

How about you?

Knock knock.

Who's there?

Ben.

Ben who?

Ben away for years but now I'm back for Christmas!

Let's party!

Knock knock.

Who's there?

Mustache.

Mustache who?

I mustache you a question.

Where did you put my presents?

Knock knock.

Who's there?

Donna.

Donna who?

Donna want to make a big deal about it but Santa is here!

Knock knock.

Who's there?

Thor.

Thor who?

My arm is very Thor from carrying this huge present!

Owwww!

Thank you so much

For reading our book.

I hope you have enjoyed these Christmas Jokes For Funny Kids as much as my kids and I did as we were putting this book together.

We really had a lot of fun and laughter creating and compiling this book and we really appreciate you for reading our book.

If you could possibly let us know what you thought of our book by way of a review we would really appreciate it 😊

To see all our latest books or leave a review just go to
kidsjokebooks.com
Once again, thanks so much for reading.
Have a very Merry Christmas!
All the best,
Jimmy Jones
And also Ella & Alex (the kids)
And even Obi (the dog – he's very cute!)

Printed in Great Britain
by Amazon

33101520R00062